For Kirsty Donbavand

First published 2016 by Walker Books Ltd
87 Vauxhall Walk, London SE11 5HJ

2 4 6 8 10 9 7 5 3 1

© 2016 Coolabi Productions Limited
Based on the Scream Street series of books by Tommy Donbavand

Based on the scripts "Mirror Mirror" by Giles Pilbrow and Ben Ward
and "Lost Looks" by Mark Huckerby and Nick Ostler.

This book has been typeset in Bembo Educational

Printed and bound in Great Britain by Clays Ltd, St Ives plc

British Library Cataloguing in Publication Data: a catalogue record for this book is available from the British Library

ISBN 978-1-4063-6786-7
www.walker.co.uk

LOOKS LIKE
TROUBLE

Tommy Donbavand

WALKER
ENTERTAINMENT

LUKE WATSON

With a troublesome taste for adventure, Luke is much like any other teenage boy – oh, except for the fact that he's also a werewolf. If he gets upset, stay well clear of him!

CLEO FARR

Cleo is a feisty teen mummy who's been in Scream Street for centuries. She's used that time to become an expert at martial arts, which comes in handy rather often.

RESUS NEGATIVE

Resus is the sarcastic son of two vampires. But he didn't get the vampire gene himself, so there's no drinking blood or turning into a bat for him – much to his disappointment.

EEFA

Thanks to a glamour spell, no one can see that the very attractive proprietor of Scream Street's neighbourhood store is really a 300-year-old witch.

ALSTON NEGATIVE

Resus's dad comes from the finest vampire bloodline, so he struggles with the idea that his son is "normal". Who wouldn't like to drink blood?

BELLA NEGATIVE

Bella, Resus's mum, is always trying to big up her son, telling him he's "special", "different" and "unique". It drives Resus nuts!

SCREAM STREET™

1 THE GHOST TRAIN

2 HAUNTED HOUSE

3 EEFA'S EMPORIUM

4 SNEER HALL

WHERE BEING A FREAK IS TOTALLY NORMAL...

5 CLEO'S HOUSE

6 THE GRAVEYARD

1 RESUS'S AND LUKE'S HOUSES

CONTENTS

Mirror, Mirror

Lost Looks

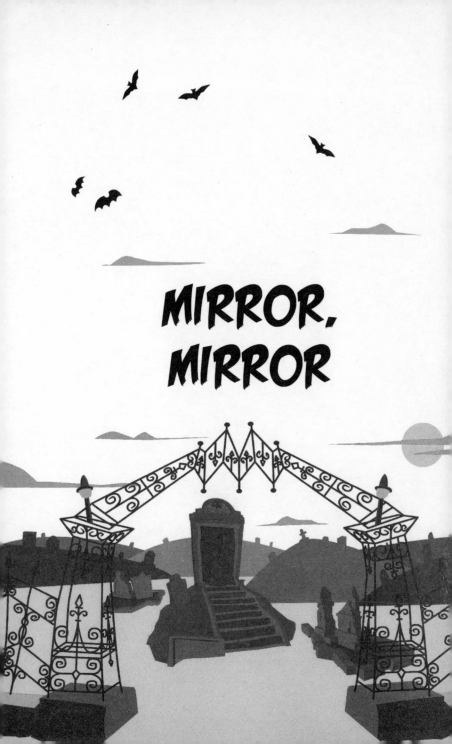

Chapter One
THE MIRROR

The blood came gushing out, looking red, sticky and delicious. With each life-giving pump of a supposedly long-dead heart, another spurt of the scarlet secretion flowed from the puncture wound and ran down the expanse of pale skin.

"Ow!" cried Alston Negative, pulling the tip of the screwdriver away from where he'd managed to stab himself in the finger. It was always the same. Human tools were made for, well, humans. And he wasn't even vaguely a member of that species.

He was a vampire.

A vampire who was taking down every mirror in the entire house.

Slipping the screwdriver into his pocket, he studied the flow of blood from the cut on his finger. The river of red was almost at his shirt cuff now and, keen as he was to simply stand and watch the life-force continue on its journey, Alston knew he would get into trouble if he caused any extra laundry for his wife.

So, flicking out a long, pointed tongue, he lapped up the blood.

He'd once been told that drinking your own blood was not good for you; it was simply recycling and not feeding. But that didn't stop the stuff from tasting incredible as it ran down the back of his throat.

"Mmmm," he said to himself. "Just like a well-preserved '67! Yummy!"

"Save some for me!" shouted Bella Negative as she speed-blurred in from the kitchen.

"Oh, I'm sorry!" said Alston. "It has all gone now." He held his clean finger out towards his wife. "But if you want to take a bite and continue from where I left off, I will happily look the

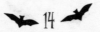

other way."

Bella scowled. "Don't tease me, Alston!" she scolded. "You know the rules of Scream Street: any vampire caught drinking blood from another living being will be banished to the Underlands."

Alston sighed. She was, of course, correct. Every vampire household in Scream Street had three taps over their kitchen sink: hot water, cold water and blood. The blood was syphoned out of the wastewater supply in the normal world, then passed through 13 different types of filtration (mainly to stop scabs getting through and causing naive vampires to choke), then plumbed into the houses.

The result was a bit like a drink labelled as "fruit flavour". All the flavours mingled together. You couldn't single out one specific blood type or taste the individual terror of someone as they held a potentially serious gushing wound over the drain.

Alston sighed. It wasn't like the old days, when you could just transform into a bat and flap out of one of the windows of your castle, bound for the throat of some terrified peasant to get the good stuff right from the source.

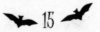 15

But then again, since the Negative family had moved to Scream Street, they hadn't opened the door to an angry mob wielding pitchforks and flaming torches even once. And no one had tried to hammer a wooden stake through his heart while he slept in his coffin.

You had to take the good with the bad.

"I still don't get it," said Bella, dragging her husband from his daytime nightmares. "Do we really have to take down the mirrors every time the relatives come over?" She held the mirror as Alston slipped a long, sharp fingernail into the head of the screw and used that to complete his task.

"I'm afraid so," he replied. "We don't want to draw attention to Resus's little, er ... problem. Remember last time, when Uncle Vlad spotted that our son had a reflection? I don't think I will ever hear the end of—"

Mr and Mrs Negative froze as they spotted their son's image in the polished surface of the mirror. He must have entered the room while they were chatting. He didn't look happy.

"Ah," said Alston, turning from the reflection to the real thing. "I didn't see you there for a moment."

"I gathered that," said Resus, flatly.

Bella blushed, her cheeks flushing from pure white to off-white. "We didn't mean..."

"Do you think I *like* having a reflection?" Resus barked.

"I'm sorry!" Bella insisted. "We didn't realize you were here..."

"Well, I am," said Resus angrily. "Even if you'd rather I wasn't!"

Alston and Bella could only share an embarrassed glance as their son stormed out of the house, slamming the front door behind him.

Outside, Resus stomped around to a small flap built into the side of the house and slumped down beside it. Reaching inside his cloak, he pulled out an ancient, rancid chicken leg and placed it on the ground near the flap. Then he produced a can of black hairspray and gave his fringe a quick blast.

Despite being born to vampire parents, Resus was something of a genetic oddity. He had naturally blond hair, wore clip-on fangs and nails, and the mere thought of drinking blood made his stomach churn.

At least his friends didn't care about his lack

of freakishness. Not like his parents. Oh, they might *say* they didn't mind hanging around for him to catch up, out of breath, after they had speed-blurred to Eefa's Emporium for tea, but he could always tell that his dad had grown bored while he waited.

More than once, he'd caught him perusing such popular magazines as *Which Witch?* and *Grossmopolitan* while he passed the time. On one occasion, Alston was halfway through a quiz to *"Find the Love Potion To Ensnare the Paranormal Creature of Your Dreams"* when Resus had finally arrived.

There was a rusty squeak as the hatch swung open and a disgusting pink leech slimed out into the open air.

"Hello, Lulu! Come on, girl!"

The animal bounded over to him and began to lick the back of his hand with a long, calloused tongue.

"At least someone loves me," said Resus quietly. He tickled the leech under what might have been her chin, then pushed himself to his feet and wandered out through the gate into Scream Street.

18

Lulu followed at full slither.

Luke Watson gripped the handle of the tennis racket and stared across the row of gravestones at his opponent. On the other side of the graveyard, Cleo Farr hopped nimbly from foot to foot and studied her competitor through the ancient Egyptian bandages that enveloped her face.

"My turn to serve," said the mummy. "Are you ready?"

Luke stood his ground, preparing himself for the oncoming match. "Ready as I'll ever be!"

"OK," said Cleo. "Here we go…"

Tossing the ball high into the air, she whacked it across the tombstones to Luke's half of the court.

Lunging to his left, Luke just managed to catch the ball with the strings of his racket and it ricocheted back towards Cleo.

She returned it with a powerful volley.

Jumping to his right this time, Luke lashed out with his racket and – *spoing!* – managed to send it flying back towards his opponent.

Smash! Cleo returned hard.

Ping! Luke was somehow able to get in the way of the ball.

Whack! The ball was shot back over the stone net at top speed.

Gah! Luke dived as far as he could, arm and racket at full stretch, but missed. He landed on the gravestone divider, half on one side of the makeshift tennis court, half on the other.

"I *think* that's another point to me," said Cleo, wincing.

Luke groaned. "You don't say," he wheezed.

Cleo nodded. "To be fair, I *have* had a bit more time to practise than you. Thousands of years more."

"Who's winning?" asked Resus, as he stepped over the court boundary, closely followed by Lulu.

"Who do you think?" grunted Luke, climbing down from the gravestone.

"Hey, Resus!" said Cleo. "What's up?"

Resus sighed hard. "Oh, you know…"

"What's up?" the mummy asked again.

"Nothing," muttered Resus, spotting the tennis ball at his feet. He tapped it with his toe, sending it rolling over towards Lulu. As it reached the leech, the ball blinked, revealing a hidden eye, then screwed itself shut again. "Apart from being an embarrassment to my whole family, that is."

"Well, I'm not exactly the son my parents wanted, either," Luke pointed out.

"At least your father doesn't hate you," said Resus.

"Your father doesn't hate you," Cleo countered. "He's just embarrassed to have you around sometimes."

Resus blinked.

"I'm not helping, am I?" Cleo asked.

"Not much, no," said Resus, shaking his head.

Luke picked up the tennis ball. "Come on," he said. "I think this is Game Over."

"Yeah," agreed Cleo. "A drink at Eefa's will cheer up Captain Gloom here."

"I doubt it," said Resus. "The way I feel right now, I wish the ground would just open up and swallow me."

The vampire took a step to follow his friends – then got his wish! He fell down, sliding through an opening in the grass and disappearing completely.

"You don't mean that, Resus," said Luke,

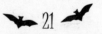

turning to smile at his friend. But there was no one there.

"Resus?" Luke and Cleo called out together.

Chapter Two
THE CRYPT

Resus crashed to the hard, stone floor of an underground crypt. Dust sprinkled down from above. The hole he'd just fallen through, which was almost impossible to see, closed up.

He climbed to his feet, brushing the dirt from his trousers, and looked around. He'd been expecting some kind of burial chamber. After all, it *was* hidden below the cemetery. But instead of coffins or sarcophagi lying around, there was nothing. In fact, if it weren't for the

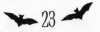

dozen or so sets of wooden shutters built into the walls of the crypt, the place would be completely empty.

Resus approached the nearest set of doors, keen to know what was behind them but also a little afraid to find out. Each set was different, as if they had been carved by different carpenters, or installed at different times. The pair of shutters he stood before now were made from a dark wood, and featured dull brass handles. He reached out and grasped a handle in each palm.

Then he hesitated. What if some eccentric family had chosen built-in cupboards as a way of storing the bodies of their loved ones? Was he just about to open a closet crammed with corpses? It wasn't that he was scared of dead bodies – some of his best friends were little more than walking cadavers – but he didn't exactly seek them out, either. If there were rotting remains behind these intricately patterned shutters, he'd be desecrating someone's grave.

But he couldn't just leave without finding out! So, taking a deep breath, he pulled the doors open wide...

...to reveal a dusty mirror. He stared at his

own repulsive reflection for the second time that morning.

"Oh, joy," he said flatly. "It's you."

"Well, it's nice to see you, too!" tutted the Resus in the mirror, folding his arms.

The real Resus blinked hard. "Huh?"

"What's the matter?" asked his reflection.

"I… I think I might have hit my head when I fell down here," Resus said, his fingers scouring his scalp for a bump. "I've just had the weirdest sensation that my reflection came alive. Oh, and now I'm talking to it. Yep, this is almost certainly a head injury."

"Don't be silly!" the reflection scoffed. "It's really me. And by me, I mean you!"

Cautiously, Resus raised a hand, and waved it back and forth. His reflection folded his arms again and smiled.

"You look really silly doing that."

Resus stuffed his hands into his trouser pockets and scowled. "No, I don't!"

"Listen," said the mirrored Resus. "It's OK, I get it. I know how much you hate having a reflection."

"Well, yes, I do," the real Resus admitted.

 25

"No offence."

"None taken," said his reflection. "But I can help you."

"Help? How?"

The reflected vampire shrugged. "Oh, it's easy. You just touch the mirror, and your reflection will be gone – for ever!"

"No way!" gasped Resus.

"Yes way!" beamed his reflection.

"But how?"

"Leave that to me," the reflection insisted. "Now, do you want to do this, or not?"

"I don't know," admitted Resus, warily. "I've seen my dad try to shave without a reflection, and it's not a pretty sight. And my mum often mucks up her make-up because she can't see what she's doing."

"Ah, yes, your parents," the reflection said, soothingly. "Proud, traditional vampires, both of them. And more than a little bit ashamed of their son. Imagine if you could get rid of me for good! The new you would be the vampire your parents always dreamed of."

"Well, it would stop my dad from cutting his finger every time Uncle Vlad decides to pop

 26

round for tea," Resus said. "OK! I suppose it can't hurt to try."

"Exactly!" said the reflection with a smile. "What have you got to lose? Now, just touch the surface of the mirror and it will all be over before you know it."

Swallowing hard, Resus reached out with his trembling fingers until the tips pressed against the cold surface of the mirror. *Whoosh*!

Resus felt himself being dragged through the glass and into the flat, terrifying world on the opposite side.

At the same time, his reflection made the journey in the opposite direction, shooting out of the mirror and landing lightly in the roomy crypt.

"Ha!" the newly released reflection laughed. "I feel so … alive!"

Behind the glass, Resus ran his palms against the surface, trying to find a way back through. But the mirror was completely solid.

"What have you done?" he cried.

"I said your reflection would be gone for ever, and I will be!" the new Resus cackled wickedly. "So long, bogus vampire!" The evil arrival reached out and grabbed the brass handles of the shutters.

"No!" screamed Resus from his polished prison cell. "Don't do this! Nooooooo!"

"Too late," snarled Evil Resus, as he slammed the doors closed. "See ya, *shampire!*"

Luke and Cleo were pacing back and forth across the area of the graveyard where Resus had disappeared. Lulu slithered unhappily between their legs.

"Don't worry, girl," said Cleo, bending to tickle the leech under her chin. "We'll find Resus, I promise." She looked up at her friend. "Luke?"

Luke was busy running the toe of his trainer through the grass, looking for clues. "What?" he replied.

"Don't you want to make Lulu feel better?"

"Oh, yeah," said Luke, focusing on the crestfallen creature. "Cheer up, Lulu."

"Not like that!" insisted Cleo. "Come over here and pet her!"

"Pet her?"

"Yes."

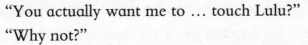

"You actually want me to … touch Lulu?"

"Why not?"

Luke cringed. "It's just that… Well, she's all slimy."

Cleo pulled a face. "Awww, is the big, bad werewolf afraid of a little bit of leech slime?"

"Of course not," protested Luke, stooping to Lulu's level. He held out a hand. "Come here, girl…"

But, before Lulu could move, there was a dark ripple in the air and Resus or something that looked exactly like him appeared in the middle of the group.

"Resus!" cried Luke, toppling backwards.

"Where did you go?" demanded Cleo.

"Why don't you come and have a look?" asked Resus, his eyes narrow.

"Are you all right, mate?" asked Luke, standing up again.

"Never better," said Resus, his tongue flicking over the tips of his fangs.

Delighted that her master was back, Lulu slithered over towards him. But she stopped a metre or so away and sniffed at the air. Then she gave out an angry *hissss!*

Resus looked down at the leech with disgust. He gave a *hisssss!* of his own, then kicked the perplexed pet away.

"Hey!" said Cleo.

Resus grabbed her arm. "I said I wanted to show you where I've been!"

"Get off!" cried Cleo. "You're hurting me!"

Luke stepped up and took Cleo's arm from Resus's painful grip. "What's going on?"

Resus looked from one friend to the other. "Maybe now's not the time," he said, to no one in particular. "I'll catch you later and that's a promise!"

Then, with a dramatic twirl of his cape, another wrinkle appeared in the air, and the vampire was gone.

"What time exactly did your brother say he would be dropping by?" asked Alston Negative as he worked to take down the final mirror in the house.

His wife shrugged. "He wasn't entirely certain he could make it," she admitted. "He said he would stop in if his anti-stakeholder's meeting finished early."

Alston sighed. "So, I've been doing all this for nothing?"

"Not for nothing," Bella said. "I mean, he might—"

The front door swung open and Resus strode confidently into the hallway.

"Resus!" cried Bella, hugging him tightly. The young vampire didn't return the embrace. "Your father wanted to say something, didn't you Alston?"

"Er, yes," said Alston, hurrying over. "What I wanted to say was … well … I mean…"

"Oh, don't worry, Dad!" said Resus, smiling wickedly, as he extracted himself from his mother's arms. "I know life has been difficult around here for a while, but things have changed. *I've* changed!"

"You have?" asked Alston. He and his wife gasped as Resus walked past one of the mirrors resting against the kitchen doorway. Their son didn't have a reflection!

By the time they looked up again, they were astonished to find him filling a glass with bright red liquid from the brass tap shaped like a pair of bat's wings.

"Lots of things are going to change around here," continued Resus. "I just need to know that, come the final reckoning, you'll be on my side."

"Well, of course," said Alston as his son raised the glass to his lips.

"Resus!" Bella cried. "You do know what that is?"

Resus raised an eyebrow, then downed the glass of blood in one go.

"What's the matter, Mother?" he asked. "Never seen a vampire drinking blood before?"

"Not this particular one, no."

Resus tossed the glass aside and wiped the blood moustache from his upper lip. "Yeah, well, I'm going to need all the strength I can get. It's going to be a long night!" He swept past them and made for the front door.

"Don't you think it's a bit late to be going out again?" Bella asked, just as the leech door swung open and Lulu peered through. The leech took one look at Resus and vanished.

"Late?" scoffed Resus over his shoulder. "Not for a vampire it isn't!"

Alston watched, open-mouthed, as his son

left. "Wow!" he said, raising the screwdriver to fix the mirror back in place. There was no need to keep them down now – even if he wasn't sure why.

Seconds later, he was sucking blood from a fresh wound on his finger.

"Ow!"

Chapter Three
THE REFLECTION

Resus's alter ego stood in the woods and took a deep breath. He had never really experienced any of his senses before, other than to watch what his lifelike counterpart was doing, and copy him in the exact opposite way. But now, he could feel the fallen twigs beneath his feet, taste the sickly sweet scent of sap on the breeze, and smell the powerfully pungent pong of decaying flesh as he wrapped his arm around the shoulders of one of Scream Street's zombies.

Doug beamed at him.

"I've got something to show you!" the fake Resus said.

The zombie's eyes grew wide, causing one of the yellowing eyeballs to fall from its socket and bounce gently against the rough, pockmarked skin of the monster's cheek, still attached to what remained of his grey matter by the optic nerve.

"Oops!" said Doug, slotting the eyeball back into place. "What is it, little vampire dude?"

"It's a surprise," hissed Resus.

"Hulawacoola!" the zombie proclaimed. "The Dougmeister *loves* surprises!"

As Resus's reflection led Doug away towards the graveyard, the zombie's pet dog, Dig, emerged from behind a tree. The animal, half flesh, half skeleton, would normally have bounded along behind them, eager to go just about anywhere. But today, the part-pooch had a feeling something wasn't quite right. So, he followed, but at a distance.

As Resus guided Doug towards the crypt, the zombie started taking guesses as to what the surprise might be.

"Is it spinal fluid?" he asked, excitedly. "'Cos if there's one thing I love more than anything else, it's that!"

"No, Doug," said Resus, making sure his chosen companion kept walking. "I'm afraid it's not spinal fluid."

"Are you sure?" questioned the zombie. "It's just that spinal fluid is all I can pretty much think about right now."

"I promise you," said Resus, with a sly smile. "It's even better than spinal fluid!"

"*Better than spinal fluid!*" Doug exclaimed. "Man, I can't even comprehend just how awesome that might be!" He froze on the spot for a second, thought hard, then fixed Resus with a hopeful stare.

"Dude, is it pus?"

In the crypt, Resus pushed Doug towards a set of shutters in the wall. These were longer than the pair of doors he'd escaped from behind, and they had bright white bones for handles.

Unseen behind them, Dig snuffled the ground at the entrance to the crypt, then poked his head in just far enough to watch what was going on.

"Go ahead," said Resus, gesturing at the

shutters. "Open them."

Doug did as he was asked, and beamed widely at the sight of his own reflection. "Hey!" he exclaimed. "Hi there, handsome duderama!"

Suddenly, the zombie behind the glass stopped copying him and leaned in. "Looking good, my man!"

"Whoa!" cried Doug, jerking backwards and sending his head tumbling from his spinal column with a *snap!* He caught the separated skull just before it hit the ground.

"Man, I've seen some weird stuff in my time," said the bodiless bonce, "but that just about takes the gall bladder!"

Click! The zombie slotted his head back in place. "It's a talking mirror!"

"Oh, it's much more than that!" hissed Resus. "Why don't you take a closer look?"

"Yeah, dude," snarled Doug's reflection. "Come closer."

"Er... That's OK," said Doug, forcing a broken-toothed smile. "I'm good."

The reflection scowled. "I said, *come closer!* Now!"

"Hey, chill out, dude!"

 37

"I'm afraid we're in kind of a hurry!" said Resus. The vampire placed his hands on the back of Doug's shoulders and pushed.

Like before, the real resident of Scream Street went tumbling through the glass surface, setting his evil counterpart free in the process.

Doug's reflection stretched as the zombie hammered on the other side of the mirror. "Hey! That's not cool! Not cool at all!"

Resus stepped forward and slammed the shutters, silencing the second captive.

Dig leapt from his hiding place, growling at the stranger who somehow looked exactly like his owner. But Doug's reflection could growl louder and scarier – and Dig was sent fleeing, his skeletal tail tucked between his bony back legs.

Evil Doug laughed, then turned back to Resus's reflection. "Right, boss," he sneered. "Who's next?"

The sun was setting by the time Cleo and Luke had finished searching the graveyard for a second time.

"There's nothing here," said Luke.

"Everything is exactly how it should be."

"Something happened to Resus, and it happened in this graveyard!" Cleo insisted. "We have to find out what."

"OK," said Luke. "But we've already covered every inch of this place."

Cleo placed her hands on her hips and looked around. "Where exactly was Resus when he disappeared?"

Luke joined his friend and pointed at the ground. "He was right about—"

The ground opened up, swallowing them both whole.

Cleo landed like a cat – on all fours, eyes darting around and ready for whatever danger was about to present itself.

Luke landed like a sack of potatoes beside her.

"Oof!"

Cleo extended a hand and helped him to his feet.

"Where are we?" Luke asked, rubbing at his back. "What is this place?"

"How should I know?"

"You're the one with a history of hanging out in underground tombs," Luke pointed out.

"If you're referring to my dad's pyramid back in Egypt, let me assure you there was a lot more gold and far fewer cobwebs!" said Cleo. She had to raise her voice towards the end of the sentence to be heard over the sound of banging.

"And it was a lot quieter, too!" she shouted. "Where's that racket coming from?"

"Over there, I think," said Luke, pointing to a pair of shutters in the far wall.

Cleo hurried over and pulled open the wooden doors without a second's hesitation. She jumped a little to find Resus staring back at her.

"Cleo!" he cried. "Thank goodness it's you!"

"Resus!" exclaimed Cleo, as Luke joined her to stare at their penned-in pal. "How did you get in there?"

"It was terrible!" yelled Resus, his breath fogging up the other side of the glass. "My dad was all 'huh' about me having a reflection, then all 'ow' when he had to take the mirrors down, and that made me feel all 'grrr' so I came to see you, Luke, but then I fell down here with an 'umph' and I opened this thing and I was, like, 'argh' 'cos there was another me, well not really another me but *another me*—"

"Slow down!" Cleo commanded. "Start again and explain it carefully."

"My reflection jumped out and trapped me," said Resus, as slowly and clearly as he could. "He's pure evil!"

While Resus continued, Luke hurried to the next set of shutters and pulled them open by their bone handles.

"Wolfie dude! Way to go!"

"Doug?"

"The one and only, Big L!"

Worried that other friends and neighbours might be trapped inside the other mirrors, Luke raced to the next pair of shutters and flung them open. This time, however, he faced his own reflection.

It winked at him.

Fascinated, Luke reached for it with trembling fingers.

"... I just touched my reflection and he swapped places with me!" Resus finished.

Cleo turned to Luke to see his reaction to the tale, but he was no longer beside her. Instead, he

41

was stretching out a hand towards—

"Luke!" Cleo bellowed. "Don't touch the mirror!"

It was too late. With a yell, the real Luke was dragged through the glass and his evil twin was ejected out into the underground tomb.

The original Luke began to hammer against the transparent wall of his dungeon. "Wait!" he cried. "No!"

"Oh, dear," said the new, naughty version. "Can't you get out?"

Behind the glass, Luke lost his temper and felt a familiar black sensation wash over him. Within seconds, his body was covered with dense hair, and fangs and long nails had sprouted, then his entire face and body changed into the shape of his inner werewolf.

The furious creature howled with rage as it smashed its furry fists repeatedly against the barrier, but the mirror held firm.

"Ha, ha, ha!" scoffed a voice. "What a loser!"

Cleo spun to see the evil versions of Resus and Doug step up to join the newly released reflection of Luke. Then they advanced on her.

"We'll have replaced the whole of Scream Street by morning!" cackled Evil Resus.

Evil Luke slammed the shutters on the real Resus, Doug and Luke, muffling their cries. Then he flipped open a new set of doors, which had lengths of knotted bandage as handles. Inside, grinning out at the assembled crowd, was Evil Cleo.

"Come to mummy!" she growled.

The renegade replicas all dashed for Cleo at once. She sprang into the air, kicking the doors of the mirror closed on her reflection. The kick enabled her to somersault over the heads of her attackers and she landed lightly behind them.

The trio of attackers spun and came at her again. Cleo aimed a flying kick at the fake Resus, but he was able to speed-blur out of her way. She karate-chopped Luke, but the wicked werewolf transformed his arm just in time to block the blow.

"Raaaaaahhh!" Cleo looked up to see Doug's double rushing for her, arms outstretched. Thinking quickly, the mummy opened the shutters to where the real Doug was trapped, then dropped onto her back. As the reflection reached her, she pushed up with her feet, sending him shooting through the glass and releasing the genuine article from the mirror.

The reflections of Resus and Luke darted towards her. Cleo twisted on the ground, then jumped up and made a run for it. They were almost upon her, when...

Doug ripped his arm off at the shoulder and hurled it after the faux fiends. The hand grabbed Luke's leg, pulling him to the ground and tripping Resus up as well.

"Cleo, run!" he yelled.

"But, Doug..."

"Don't worry about me! You get to safety."

The reflections of her two best friends climbed to their feet and grabbed Doug, dragging him back to the mirror and pushing him through it.

"I'll be back!" she cried out, as she raced for the exit. "I'll be back to save you all!"

Chapter Four
THE PLAN

Cleo lay flat on top of the tallest tomb in the graveyard, and peered out over the moonlit pavements of Scream Street.

The evil reflections of Luke, Resus and Doug were clearly searching for her. They met first outside Eefa's in the central square, then each explored two or three side streets before gathering together again.

"Think, Cleo, think!" she hissed to herself. "I can't ask anyone for help, because I don't know

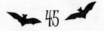

who else those creeps have swapped with."

Suddenly she felt a wet patch spreading over the bandages on her left cheek. Lulu the leech was nuzzling up against her. Cleo patted the creature on the top of her head. She began to purr with a noise that sounded like someone blowing bubbles in a bowl of custard.

"It'll be OK, girl," Cleo promised. "I've got a plan. But I'm going to need your help."

Purrrggglle!

"That's exactly what I wanted to hear," said Cleo with a smile. "Now, let's gather what we need and get to it!"

Hoo-hoo!

An owl settled silently onto a branch in the woods, its huge eyes focused on the juicy mouse scrambling through the undergrowth below. The bird had spread its wings, and was readying itself to pounce, when a gnarled mouth opened up in the tree trunk and swallowed the owl whole.

The mouse scurried towards home as the tree coughed out a mouthful of feathers.

Cleo picked her way through the under-growth, pausing only to brush a falling feather from her shoulder. She heard a *crack* – someone stepping on a twig behind her. She tried very hard not to smile.

"Oh, no!" she said loudly. "One of my shoelaces has come untied." She glanced down and added to herself, "Which is particularly strange, since I don't wear shoes."

Still, she dropped to one knee and rearranged the bandages that covered her foot.

With a furious *roar*, Evil Luke dashed out from behind a tree and charged straight for her. Cleo raced off through the woods ahead of him.

"There's no point running!" Luke's reflection shouted. "We'll get you, and we won't be beaten!"

Cleo slowed her pace a little. She didn't want to be too far ahead of her pursuer when she…

…burst through the leaves of an overhanging branch and grinned at the sight ahead of her. It was the mirror containing the real Luke, removed from the underground crypt and nailed to a tree.

Cleo jumped, placing her foot just above the mirror, and flipped over backwards. As she spun, she reached down and deftly opened the shutters of the mirror with one hand.

"No!" snarled Luke's reflection, seeing his opposite suddenly appear ahead of him. The copy tried to stop, but tripped over something bulky hidden under the leaves – Lulu!

The monster flew towards the mirror, disappearing through the glass and releasing the real Luke from captivity.

Cleo appeared at his side, taking his hand and helping him up. "Nice to have you back," she beamed.

Inside the mirror, Luke's reflection hammered on the glass with his fists. "I'll get out," he bellowed, "and when I do—"

Luke slammed the shutters closed. "Yeah, yeah." He dusted off his hands and gave Cleo a high-five. "One down…"

"…two to go!"

Doug's double staggered down a side road towards the central square. What was left of his mind was racing with the possibilities of finally being free.

He'd been trapped inside the mirror ever since the real Doug had clawed his way out of a freshly filled grave and first glanced at his rancid reflection. The result had been quite a shock for both of them. Not only was there the advanced stage of decomposition to contend with – Doug had lost his hand for the first time trying to smash through his coffin lid – but there was also the fact that neither of them could remember who they had been before the visit from the grim reaper.

The real Doug had staggered around the cemetery for a while, looking for clues as to his former identity. He had spotted a young couple laying flowers at a new gravestone near the gates, and he'd tried calling out to them for help.

Unfortunately, due to not having used his vocal chords for however long he'd spent underground, his friendly greeting of "Good morning!" came out sounding more like "Glark!"

The couple had run, screaming, as he shambled towards them.

By the time it occurred to him to read the name on the tombstone beneath which he'd just emerged, a team of featureless Movers was closing in on him from all sides. The next thing he knew, he was being shipped off to Scream Street.

But now that Doug was gone, and the new, improved version was stalking the streets. The new, improved version had all of Doug's charm and good looks, but none of that pesky morality that had always kept the original from achieving his potential.

Like most zombies, the real Doug enjoyed eating body fluids, but he didn't believe the undead should attack the living – or in some cases the almost living – to satisfy their thirst. Instead, he waited for a healthy glob of goo to be dumped in the bins around the back of Eefa's or donated by a newly deceased neighbour.

Then he did something no other walking corpse could understand. He cooked the glop before eating it! Preferably with some spices, and a bottle of bile to wash it all down. Doug's reflection shuddered at the thought. Disgusting!

Now that he was free, he could get his fill of body bits straight from the source. Every single one of these houses on either side of the road had residents sleeping in them, with bulging, juicy guts just waiting to be devoured. Ideally while still attached to a living, yet terrified, nervous system! There was nothing like fear to add flavour to an unwilling meal.

Evil Doug heard his stomach growl or perhaps

it was the badger that had recently taken up residence in the space where his liver used to be. Either way, the reflection was hungry. He wanted to feed, and he knew exactly what he was after.

"Aaaaaaaah!" cried Cleo as convincingly as she could, which wasn't very.

The zombie's head snapped up. There she was! The mummy! The trouble-maker! The source of his next meal!

Evil Doug gave chase, picking up speed as he ran across the central square. His prey disappeared around a corner – which led to a dead end. Ha! A dead end! How fitting! If he had still owned a complete set of salivary glands, they would have been working overtime.

Licking his cracked lips, the dangerous double dashed into the cul-de-sac, just in time to see Luke step out into view, holding an ornate set of shutters in his hands. Cleo dropped and skidded between her friend's legs.

Doug didn't know what they were planning and, frankly, he didn't care. Somehow the goody-goody version of Luke had escaped, but that just meant there were seconds on the menu! He hurried forward…

… and stepped right onto the back of Lulu. The leech skidded in her own gloop, sending Doug sliding towards the shutters, just as Luke pulled them open to reveal the mirror. The Xeroxed zombie was out of control!

He managed to slam his palms against the wooden sides of the looking glass, stopping his forward momentum and avoiding returning to his prison.

Cleo and Luke exchanged a worried glance.

"Better luck next time," Evil Doug snarled.

Then Dig leapt out from behind a hedge and bit the crazed copy hard on the bottom.

"Yeeeooowww!"

Doug's reflection screamed as he bounded forward, slipping back into the mirror and releasing his harmless opposite.

"Nice move, half-doggie dude!" beamed Doug, as Dig scampered over to lick his leathery cheek.

Luke slammed the doors of the mirror shut.

Cleo cracked her neck from side to side. "Let's wrap this!" she said with a grin.

Chapter Five
THE CHOICE

Cleo stood in the central square, bathed in moonlight, and slowly turned a full 360 degrees. She'd been there for almost 10 minutes. So far, there was no sign of Resus's reflection.

While she felt encouraged that she'd managed to help Luke and Doug escape from their mirrors, she knew that freeing Resus wouldn't be easy. The alternate, wicked version of him had been waiting to emerge for a long time, and he wasn't going to go back without a fight.

She spun on the spot again, but the square remained deserted.

She almost felt sorry for the reflections, trapped behind a pane of glass, only seeing the light of day when someone stumbled across the hidden, underground crypt where the mirrors were stored.

Perhaps, she—

"Waiting for someone?"

Cleo jumped at the voice. It was close. Very close. Almost whispering in her ear. She turned around to find Resus's reflection just a few metres away.

"I keep forgetting that you can speed-blur," she said, trying not to show that she had been given a shock.

"I can do everything that fake-fanged friend of yours can't!" Evil Resus sneered. "And I don't mope about the house, trying to avoid anything dangerous and wetting my pants at the first sign of trouble."

Cleo folded her arms. "So, what exactly do *you* get up to in your spare time?"

"There won't *be* any spare time when I've finished," the bogus vampire spat. "Monsters will be monsters again – scary, nasty, evil! No more hiding away in magically protected communities for us! Once I have released the reflection of everyone in Scream Street, we'll take on the outside world and send the normals running for their lives!"

"Sounds like you'll be busy," said Cleo. "But you're forgetting just one thing."

"And what's that?"

"To do any of that, you'll have to get through me first!"

Evil Resus threw his head back and laughed. "You never learn, do you?" he cackled. "I can get through you as easy as my fangs can get through the skin of a normal's throat!"

Cleo raised an eyebrow. "You haven't had much luck so far."

"Luck can change," sneered the vampire. He raised a hand and clicked his fingers. Two figures — Luke and Doug — stepped out of the shadows to stand behind their leader. They both scowled hard at the sight of Cleo.

"You, like, summoned us, boss dude?" Doug growled.

"I most certainly did," replied Resus's reflection.

Luke screwed his eyes closed for a second. The bones in his knuckles cracked as his palms flooded with thick dense hair. Long talons erupted from his fingertips, completing the change from human hands to powerful werewolf paws. "What do you want us to do?"

Evil Resus narrowed his eyes, but kept his gaze fixed on Cleo. "Unfortunately, the mummification process has already taken many of her internal organs, but there are still enough bits in there to have fun with. Let's take her apart!"

As the vampire stepped forward, Luke and Doug grabbed his arms tightly.

"I don't think so!" Luke hissed.

Resus's reflection struggled to free himself from their grasp. "What's going on?"

"Karma!" said Doug brightly. "That's what's going on! You're going to get what you deserve, little bad dude!"

Cleo put her hands on her hips and smiled. "Surprise!" she said, as she stepped up to the vampire villain and took Doug's place.

The zombie reached behind a dustbin and produced a large wooden frame that surrounded a pair of closed shutters. Old brass handles glinted in the moonlight.

"It's time to take a long, hard look in the mirror!" said Cleo.

"No!" cried Evil Resus, pushing backwards with his feet. "Not that thing. I'm *not* going back inside there! You don't know what it's like!"

Luke increased his grip on his faux friend. "Actually, we do," he said. "Thanks to you!" Then he and Cleo began to push Resus's reflection back towards where it had first appeared.

"No! Noooooo!"

Suddenly, the air seemed to shimmer and two new figures appeared, standing directly between Evil Resus and the mirror.

It was Mr and Mrs Negative.

"Put my son down!" commanded Alston.

"Sure thing, Mr Scary Vampire dude," said Doug, lowering the mirror to the ground.

"Not you!" said Alston. "Them!"

Luke and Cleo released their grip on Evil Resus. He speed-blurred over to his parents and hugged his mum.

Bella stroked his hair gently. "Good job we came to check on you," she said. "Are you all right?"

"I am now that you're here … Mother!" Resus crooned.

"Mrs Negative," said Cleo, stepping forward. "That's *not* your son."

"What are you talking about?" demanded Alston. "Of course that's our son!"

"No, it's not," said Luke. "It just looks like him."

Cleo crossed to the mirror and opened the shutters. "Here's your *real* son."

Alston and Bella Negative peered at the vampire slumped unhappily behind the glass.

"Hi Mum, hi Dad!" said the real Resus.

Alston looked from one young vampire to the other. "Resus?"

"What is going on here?" exclaimed Bella.

"It's him!" said Resus, pointing out of his polished prison. "He's my reflection! He trapped me in here, and then tried to do the same to everyone else."

"Don't listen to him," Evil Resus scoffed. "He's obviously *my* reflection. Look, he's in a mirror, for garlic's sake!"

"Yes, but I'm not copying your every move, am I?" pointed out the original Resus.

"Only because you don't have the guts!" barked his carbon copy.

"Stop! Stop!" cried Alston. "This is all very confusing!"

"How are we supposed to tell which Resus is which?" wailed Bella.

The reflection hugged her. "You've got the genuine article right here," he said, staring up at her with wide eyes. "You know it's really me!"

"Dad, don't believe him!" said the vampire in the mirror. "I'm the real Resus Negative! You have to make him touch the mirror so I can get out of here!"

Mr and Mrs Negative looked at each other, baffled.

"I *think* that's the real Resus in there," said Alston, pointing to the mirror. "Or, it could be that one hugging you!"

"Well, I'm sure this one is Resus," said Bella, pulling the vampire in her arms even closer. "Unless, of course, the one in the mirror is telling the truth."

Doug poked his head up from behind the dustbins. "I'm starting to get a little confused, too," he admitted. "Am I still Doug?"

Cleo ignored the zombie and turned to the mirror. "You have to believe us," she said to the older vampires. "This is your son."

"And I know just how he can prove it," said Luke.

"What?" said both Resuses at the same time. "How?"

A smile crept across Luke's face. "We are standing here arguing over who is the real Resus, but what we should be asking is... Who is the real vampire?"

The Resus in the mirror grinned. "Of course!" he cried, reaching up to remove his false fangs. "Look, it's me!"

"Resus!" exclaimed Bella and Alston. They turned to scowl at their son's reflection, who began to back away.

"Now, hold on!" said the double. "Why would you want him back when you've got the new and improved version right here? I can drink blood, speed-blur..." He whizzed up to Alston and raised an eyebrow. "No need for mirrors all over the house. I'm just like the old model, only much, much better!"

Alston nodded. "He's got a point."

"What?" barked Bella.

"Well," said Alston, "he does seem, you know, a bit more … vampirey!"

Resus hammered on the other side of the mirror. "Dad, no!"

Cleo fought back her tears. "Mr Negative, you can't!"

Alston shrugged. "There wouldn't be any more problems when the family comes around."

"Please, Mr Negative," begged Luke. "Don't do this!"

Resus's evil twin smiled wickedly at them all. "Too late, losers! He's made his choice."

"Indeed, I have!" said Alston.

Evil Resus gazed up at his new father and licked the tips of his fangs with his tongue. "Aren't I just the son you always wanted?"

Alston wrapped an arm around the boy's shoulders. "The son I always wanted," he said slowly and carefully, "is the one I've got already!"

With that, he picked up the fake Resus and hurled him into the mirror. The real article came flying out, landing with a thump at his parents' feet.

61

Luke and Cleo slammed the shutters over the mirror to muffle the furious screams coming from within, just as Lulu slithered up to squirm happily over her master's shoes.

Alston hugged his son tightly. "We wouldn't change you for the world!"

Resus buried his face in Alston's cloak as Bella joined the embrace. "Oh, Dad! Mum!"

Cleo wiped her eyes with the bandages on her hand. Luke gave her a nudge. "Getting soppy in your old age, are you?"

"Hulawacoola!" came a cry, as Doug leapt out from behind the bins. "Group hug!"

The zombie wrapped his skinny arms around the entire Negative family and squeezed tight. One of his eyeballs popped out and swung on its length of optical nerve.

"Oops!" Doug chuckled. "I think I might have ruined the moment, dudes. My bad!

Totally my bad!"

LOST LOOKS

Chapter One
THE ATTIC

The dustbin stank. A foul odour emanated from hunks of rotten, decomposing meat, and even fouler liquids worked their way down through an assortment of discarded spell books, shattered crystal balls and boxes of toads' tongues that were well past their sell-by date.

By the time the vile juices reached the bottom of the bin, they were infused with all kinds of malevolent magic and putrid powers – and that was how the rats liked them.

The rats of Scream Street emerged, blinking and squealing, from the sewers every rubbish collection day. For one day a week, their menu was upgraded from whatever tiny, unsuspecting creatures they could catch in the sludgy waste pipes to an incredible assault upon the senses. Delicious debris, succulent scraps and luscious leftovers were waiting at the end of every garden path.

But the rats weren't the only predators who took to the hunt on bin day. Another figure, this one sleek, curved and wearing a blood-orange dress, scoured the bins, looking for just the right size and shape of...

Aha!

Eefa Everwell, Scream Street's most powerful witch and owner of the community's emporium, plunged a hand down into the clammy contents of one of the bins outside her store's back door. Long, slender fingers tipped with perfectly manicured scarlet nails worked their way through the slime until they found what they were looking for.

"Got you!" cried Eefa, as she pulled a large rat out of the rubbish. The rodent was long, plump and furious. It wriggled and squealed, desperate to free itself from the witch's grasp, teeth gnashing and long, pink tail twisting.

But Eefa wasn't about to let go of her prize. This one would keep her stocks topped up for at least a week.

Slipping back inside the store, she hurried to a spot on the shop counter where three glasses stood, each containing a dose of thick strawberry syrup. Making sure no one could see what she was doing, she held up the squirming rat and whispered a spell beneath her breath. Instantly, the rat began to squirt out streams of sickly sweet milk, which Eefa was careful to ensure topped up each of the three waiting glasses. The task complete, she popped the rat into the refrigerator and rewarded it with a slice of mouldy cheese, which was received with gratitude.

Finally, Eefa popped a straw into each of the pink frothy drinks and sent them floating to a table occupied by three customers.

"Oh, wicked! Another milkshake!" exclaimed Luke Watson, as one of the glasses settled in front of him. He noisily downed the last of his previous shake, slid the empty receptacle aside

69

and began to devour its replacement.

"I don't know how Eefa does it," the vampire sitting beside him announced as he regarded his own milky beverage. "Her shakes are the best!" Resus Negative removed the pair of fake fangs that were clipped to his top teeth and sucked hard on his straw.

The only occupant of the table who didn't start on her drink straight away was Egyptian mummy Cleo Farr, and that was only because she was peering between the shop shelves towards a trio of figures standing near a large mirror on the far wall.

"I don't believe it," she giggled. "He's doing it again!"

Luke and Resus twisted in their seats to watch as the mayor of Scream Street, Sir Otto Sneer, paraded vainly up and down in front of the mirror.

"Ah, such beauty!" he proclaimed. "Such perfection!"

The mayor's trainee assistant, Dixon, looked around eagerly. "Where?"

"Here, you fool!" barked Sneer. "I ask you, do I look like I *need* pimple potions, wrinkle removers and wart sprays?"

Dixon blinked. "Is this a trick question, boss?"

"Bah!" Otto pushed past his assistant to where Eefa's niece, Luella, was standing, arms folded, chewing gum and utterly bored.

"What do you think?"

Suddenly jerked back to reality, Luella shook her head and hoped that she could answer the question correctly. "OMG, of course not," she said. "You're, like, really, really handsome."

She fixed a smile on her face and sighed. Eefa had recently been trying to teach her that "the customer is always right". Apparently, that included customers who flounced up and down in front of their own reflection, complimenting themselves.

Dixon sidled up to his boss and spoke quietly. "It's just that, as you're having your portrait painted today, Mr Sneer, sir, I thought you might like to look your best."

There was a brief, awkward silence.

"And by that, sir," Dixon quickly added, "I mean even more stunning than usual!"

"Hmmm," mused Otto. "Well, maybe just

a little something then." With a sweep of his arm, the mayor cleared the entire shelf of beauty products, burying his assistant beneath an avalanche of bottles, sprays and potions.

"Good choices, sir," he groaned.

Back at the table, Resus was giggling so much that strawberry milk was starting to dribble out of his nostrils. "He bought the lot!" he gasped.

Luke patted his friend on the back. "Just imagine him, preening himself!"

"Ssshh," hissed Cleo. "He's coming this way!"

Otto paused long enough at the counter to toss his credit card – a platinum G.H.O.U.L. Monstercard – in front of Luella. "Make sure Dixon remembers the receipt," he grunted, then made for the door.

Thonk!

His bulbous behind got stuck as he tried to stride through the exit. It took a bit of wiggling for the mortified mayor to free himself and hurry away.

It was Luke's turn to spit out milkshake as he laughed. The pink spray coated the table top

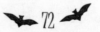

and most of Cleo's bandages.

"Hey!" she cried, grabbing the corner of Resus's cloak and wiping herself down.

"Sorry," wheezed Luke, when he could speak again. "But that … was … *fantastic!*"

"I know," said Cleo with a grin. "Otto's having a portrait painted? All the beauty routines in the world won't help him!"

"A face transplant might," Resus suggested.

The air beside Luke sparkled and Eefa shimmered into view. She was holding a cloth and scowling down at the milky mess covering the table. "And which of you is going to clean up this mess?" she asked.

"I will!" said Luke, snatching the cloth and gazing up at her. He knew that Eefa wore an enchantment charm to improve her appearance, but that had never mattered to him. Ever since he had first moved to Scream Street, he had admired her powerful personality, her expertise with magic and her … amazing red hair, flawless porcelain skin and pouting crimson lips. And those unbelievable eyes! He could just stare deep into her eyes for days at a time and never need to emerge for—

"Hello? Earth to Luke?" Cleo was snapping her fingers in front of his face.

Luke jumped. "Huh?"

Cleo winked at Resus. "I thought we'd lost him there for a minute!"

"Yeah," Resus chuckled. "Enchanted by Eefa!"

"Don't be daft!" Luke snapped. "I was just … thinking of something, that's all."

"We could tell," Cleo grinned, arching an eyebrow towards the winsome witch, who was helping Luella pack Sir Otto's purchases into a bag for Dixon.

"No, not that," Luke scoffed. "Honestly, I don't know why people seem to be obsessed with looks today. It's so shallow!"

"It is?" asked Resus.

"Definitely!" Luke replied. "It's not what someone looks like that counts. The important part is what's underneath."

"What's underneath where?" demanded Eefa, melting into view again.

Luke's cheeks flushed. "Underneath… Er, that is… You know…" He swallowed hard and held out the cloth, dripping strawberry milkshake

74

onto the carpet. "I finished cleaning the table."

"So I can see," said Eefa, wryly. "I don't suppose you want to help me clean my attic as well, do you?"

"Of course!" said Luke, eyes fixed on the witch's beautiful eyes once more. "I'll do it! Count me in!"

Eefa flashed Luke a stunning smile and handed him a broom before turning and slinking away. Luke watched her leave and sighed.

"You're so lucky you're not obsessed with looks," said Cleo.

Luke turned to her. "What?"

"You're a liar, Luke Watson. You've so got the hots for Eefa!"

"I have not!" Luke countered. "I... I just thought that helping her, you know, clean up would be a nice, neighbourly thing to do."

Cleo folded her arms. "Oh, yeah?"

"Yeah," said Luke. "And hey, a witch's attic, guys! I bet there's some pretty cool stuff up there." With that, he jumped up and hurried after Eefa.

"Bad excuse," Cleo said to Resus, "but he might be right. Are you in?"

"Fine," said Resus, clipping his fake fangs back into place. "But if he starts to get all drooly again, I am out of here!"

Chapter Two
THE PORTRAIT

Luke clambered up the wooden stairs to the attic at the top of Eefa's Emporium – then stopped and stared. All along one wall were shelving units packed with boxes of wands, crystal balls, and all manner of weird and wonderful potions. There was a stack of framed pictures resting against the side of the shelves, a collection of dried plants and animal parts in variously sized glass jars, and a large sack that appeared to have something – or some*things* – wriggling around inside.

"Whoa! Are you sure you want to throw all this stuff away?" he asked, as Eefa shimmered into existence beside him. "It looks brilliant!"

Cleo and Resus arrived to study the collection. The mummy grabbed the buzzing handle of one of several witch's brooms while her friend reached out to flip open an ancient book of spells.

Resus jumped as the book gave out a *growl*, then snapped down on his fingers, trapping them.

"Waaah!" he cried.

Eefa waved her hand over the book, forcing it to release the vampire. Then she grabbed the top of Luke's head and spun him around to face the other direction. The other side of the attic was strewn with rubbish bags, shards of broken skulls, torn parchments and more.

"This is the side of the attic I want you to clean," she said. "Don't touch anything on the other side – that's extra merchandise I can't fit into the stockroom."

But Luke wasn't paying attention. He was running his hand through his hair, rubbing at the spot where the witch's beautiful long, red fingernails had touched his scalp. He was never going to shower, ever—

"Luke, are you listening to me?"

"Er, yeah!" said Luke, pushing his hand deep into his pocket. "Of course. You were, er … talking about this stuff over here." He took a step towards the filthy side of the room, tripped over a box of out-of-date memory worms and crashed to the ground in a billowing cloud of dust.

He quickly jumped up again, covered in dirt but trying his hardest to keep his cool. "So, yeah," he said. "I was just checking the old floor there and, yes, it needs sweeping."

Then he sneezed.

Eefa handed over a broom and made for the stairs. "The bins are collected at noon," she said. "There's an extra-large milkshake in it for each of you if this place is tidy by then."

Resus and Cleo shared a high-five, then started stuffing bits of rubbish into bags. It was a few minutes before they realized that Luke wasn't moving. He was rooted to the spot, staring at the empty space at the top of the stairs where Eefa had just been.

"You do know she's, like, three hundred years old, don't you?" asked Resus.

Luke jumped, the spell broken. "What? No, you've got it all wrong. I don't like Eefa!"

Cleo didn't look convinced.

Luke started to sweep the floor energetically. "Even if I did, that's got nothing to do with me wanting to help her clean up. I just love dust, and spiders' webs, and more dust, and… Wow, there's so much dust!"

Within seconds there was dust everywhere. Resus covered his head with his cape and coughed.

Cleo pulled her bandages down over her eyes and coughed.

The spell book on the shelf ruffled its pages and coughed.

Luke dropped the broom and stumbled backwards, his eyes stinging. He bumped into something and heard it clatter to the floor.

Eventually, Cleo managed to stagger over to a small window and open it. Gradually, the cloud of dust dissipated, allowing Luke to see that he had knocked over one of the portraits. He picked it up…

… causing Resus to scream and disappear back beneath his cloak.

"What's the matter, Resus?" Cleo asked. She moved to where the vampire was pointing with a trembling finger and looked at the portrait.

"Oh, my stink beetles!" she cried. "Who – or what – is that?"

"I don't know," came Resus's muffled reply. "But, whoever it is, someone should cover that face with bandages. No offence."

"Some taken," said Cleo. "Why would Eefa hold on to something quite so hideous?"

Luke turned the painting around so that he could study the subject. He paled.

"Yikes!" he said. "Looks like someone fell out of the ugly tree – and hit every single branch on the way down!"

The picture was of a woman with wrinkled green skin, a long pointed nose, squinting purple eyes and lank greasy hair. Her teeth were broken and yellow, and she was covered in more warts than should ever be allowed to gather together in one place.

"Has it gone yet?" squeaked Resus.

"Almost," said Luke, pushing the portrait

into a rubbish bag and tying it up tight. "This one's definitely for the bin!"

Grabbing the top of the bag, he swung it round and tossed it out the window.

"Look out below!"

Dixon scowled as he stomped out of Sneer Hall. "Go and get more wrinkle cream, Dixon," he grumbled, trying to imitate his boss. "Shampoo my hair, Dixon. Shave my knees, Dixon."

He paused, looking around to make sure no one had overheard him. He didn't like being treated like a servant by Otto, but he couldn't imagine what would happen if anyone told the mayor that he had been ridiculing him.

Dixon had always dreamed of one day rising to a position of power and importance. And if that meant becoming rich and famous as a result, then he would just have to put up with that.

As a toddler, he'd used his shapeshifting powers to transform into identical copies of his fellow pre-schoolers in order to get their share of milk and snacks.

At school, he would occasionally impersonate

Dr Skully, Scream Street's skeletal teacher, to fool his classmates into handing over their answers to particularly difficult homework quizzes.

His tricks had backfired, however, when he had imitated Acrid Belcher, the former head of Government Housing of Unusual Lifeforms (known as G.H.O.U.L.). In this guise, he had attempted to launch his latest "invention": instant boots – footwear that does the walking for you! In reality, they were just a pair of old wellies with a secondhand animation spell cast over them, but that wasn't where his plan unravelled. In fact, things were going well until he was invited to an interview by *The Terror Times*.

Dixon had confidently marched into the newspaper's headquarters, only to discover that the *real* Acrid Belcher was now the editor – and he wanted to know why there were suddenly two of him in the world! In a panic, Dixon quickly hid by shifting into the shape of an office chair, and spent the following three days being sat on by an overweight troll sports reporter before he could finally escape.

So when the opportunity to become the

trainee-assistant-deputy-intern to the mayor had arisen, Dixon had jumped at the chance. No more pretending to be other people to get the lifestyle he wanted. Now he could sample the good life for real.

Only, it hadn't turned out that way. All Otto Sneer wanted was a body to fetch and carry for him. Someone to do his dirty work, literally. And that poor sap was Dixon.

"I'd like to tell him exactly what to do with this job," he muttered as he approached Eefa's. "If I wasn't so very scared of him, that is!"

Crash!

The bag of rubbish that Luke had thrown out the window landed at his feet, splitting open as it collided with the pavement.

"Aarrgh!"

Dixon jumped, certain that Otto was right behind him with another missile to launch at his sassy subordinate. But the street was deserted.

Once his heart stopped thumping, Dixon made for the shop entrance again, but his attention was caught by the corner of a picture frame sticking out of the bag. He pulled it out to study it.

"Nice frame!" he said to himself. "This will be perfect for Otto's new portrait! I'll bet he gives me a pay rise to *real* money when he sees this!"

Then, he turned the painting over and glanced at the hideous hag on the other side. "I won't get it if he's sees this bit, though! Yuck!"

Tearing the picture from the frame, he tossed the putrid painting over his shoulder and marched back towards Sneer Hall, just as a team of farting goblins wheeled a cart over to the bins and collected the bags of rubbish.

"There!" said Eefa, sending three Chocolate Surprise milkshakes floating over to the table where Luke, Resus and Cleo were waiting. "That's for doing such a good job."

Luke grinned. "It's no problem," he said, gazing over at the witch. "And, if anything else needs doing, just ask me. Us. But mostly me."

Blushing, he raised his glass ... and poked himself in the eye with the straw. That didn't stop him staring at Eefa with the other eye, however.

"He's at it again," Resus hissed. "I think I'm going to be sick!"

Luke opened his mouth to reply but, before he could say anything, a horrified scream rang out from behind the counter. The trio watched as Eefa covered her face with her hands, then ran up the stairs, slamming the door behind her.

"Looks like you're not the only one," said Cleo.

Chapter Three
THE FRAME

"Can I look now? *Pleeeaaassse?*"

Otto Sneer twisted round from his "I'm heroic, yet accessible" pose on the grand staircase of Sneer Hall and looked towards a paintbrush flicking back and forth by itself in the air. The tip made sudden dabs and strokes onto a large canvas resting on an easel.

Occasionally, an artist's palette hovered into view, and the brush plunged its bristles into a different colour of paint before resuming work.

This was the world's great poltergeist painter, Millicent van Cough.

"I just want a little peek," Otto groaned.

"Silence!" screeched the invisible artist, jabbing her brush in the mayor's direction. "I have painted the most beautiful and glamorous people this world has ever seen! I was the artist who immortalized in oil that great skeleton dictator, Napoleon Bony-Parts. I was the one who really gave *The Scream* a fright. And who else could be responsible for the greatest ever portrait of that wailing banshee, *The Moaning Lisa*?"

Otto sighed. "But—"

"No buts!" insisted the poltergeist. "Millicent van Cough *never* shows her work until it is perfect."

A second passed.

"OK, it's perfect!"

The easel spun to show Otto the finished portrait. His jaw dropped open.

"I know, eh?" said Millicent. "Ta-da!"

Otto stumbled down the great staircase and approached the painting, hoping against hope that there had been some mistake. Perhaps Millicent van Cough had accidentally been looking out of the window and caught a goblin in mid-fart instead. From behind. Close up.

The picture was a mass of swirling greens and greys. There were features, of course, like eyes (too close together), ears (large and sticking out) and a mouth (which appeared to show the mayor in the process of sucking leech slime from a thistle).

"Do... Do I really look like that?" he croaked.

Millicent was busy packing away her paints and brushes. She paused – or at least Otto thought she did. "What can I say? You're no oil painting."

Then the paint set lifted up into the air and floated out of the window.

Otto gazed at his portrait and sighed. Maybe he should have opened that extra bottle of pimple cream, after all.

He turned and trudged away in the direction of the bathroom, just as Dixon hurried in with the ornate frame. He spotted the finished painting, and hurried over to take a peek.

"Aargh!" he cried. "She's captured his likeness perfectly! Otto won't like that at all. Hmm... Maybe a new frame will help take the edge off what's on the canvas."

Dixon slotted the frame over the portrait, blinking hard as the wooden mount seemed to shimmer for a second. Then he lifted the finished picture off the easel, and hung it on the wall.

He stepped back to admire his handiwork, then jumped as a piercing *scream* rattled the windows and doors.

"Oh, my goodness!" bellowed a voice. "My face!"

"Oh, no," said Dixon to himself, as he hurried up the staircase. "Otto's gone and had a proper look at himself in the mirror! I knew this portrait was a bad idea!"

Dixon crashed into the bathroom to find Otto staring at his own reflection. "Now, don't you worry, Mr Sneer, sir," he said. "I'm sure there's a cosmetic surgeon somewhere who doesn't mind working with hopeless causes. All we need to do is—"

His lips continued to flap open and closed as the mayor turned to face him, but no sound came out.

"Well, Dixon?" demanded Sir Otto. "Like what you see?"

Dixon stared. The figure standing in front of him was still Otto Sneer, but a much younger, more handsome version. Gone were the pock-marked cheeks and balding scalp. In their place was healthy, taut skin and a head of hair so thick and luxurious that the mayor looked as if he'd just stepped off the set of an ad for expensive shampoo.

Otto ran his fingers through his quiff, allowing a single cheeky curl to drop down over one eye.

Dixon felt his legs turn to jelly. "Wh-what happened, Mr Sneer, sir?" he croaked.

"Why, nothing at all, Dixon!" came the reply. "Except that I'm *perfect*!"

Luella looked up from her cauldron as yet another unhappy customer stomped – well, slimed – over to Eefa's counter.

"I want a refund!" demanded Mr Crudley, slamming a bottle down in front of the young witch. "This was supposed to be an indigestion remedy!"

Luella looked blankly back at the angry bog monster. "And...?"

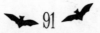

"And?" roared Mr Crudley. "And? And it makes you breathe fire!" Stooping, he fed a mouthful to Dig, the half-skeletal dog that roamed Scream Street. The pooch gulped down the potion eagerly, then he burped a fireball, and a cloud of black smoke emerged from his bony back-end.

"So, you don't want it, then?" asked Luella.

"Of course I don't want it!" gurgled the bog monster. "I've just spent the past twenty minutes trying to extinguish a blaze on my armchair!"

The door to the stockroom slammed open. Luke, Resus and Cleo came racing out, arms piled high with bottles. They dumped them next to Luella.

"Here are the ingredients you asked for," said the mummy, trying to catch her breath.

Luella snatched up the nearest bottle and scowled at the label. "No, I said liquidized *tongue of rat* not *lung of bat*! If I make anything out of that, half of Scream Street will be finding their way around with ultrasonic squeaks by the end of the day!"

"Sorry," said Cleo. "It's quite dark back there, and hard to see what's—"

Before she could finish, Bella Negative pushed her way to the front of the queue. "This vampire sunscreen is actually an invisibility potion!" she snapped, rubbing a blob of the cream into the skin of her arm.

Luella gasped as Mrs Negative's arm disappeared before her very eyes. "OMG, I'm, like, so sorry," she said. "I'll mix another batch up just as soon as—"

"Oh, I don't have time to wait!" cried Bella. Tossing the bottle into the bin, she turned and stormed out of the shop.

Resus dashed around the counter to retrieve it from the rubbish. "Might come in handy the next time I feel like disappearing," he said, with a wink to Luke.

Bang!

Everyone ducked as the concoction in Luella's cauldron exploded. Well, everyone except Luella, that is. When Luke, Resus and Cleo clambered back to their feet, the young witch was still stirring the charred handle of her wooden spoon in the air. Her purple hair was sticking straight up, and both of her eyebrows had been blasted off.

93

"Yikes!" said Resus, then "Oof!" as Cleo elbowed him in the ribs before he could say anything else.

"Erm, guys," said Luella, quietly. "Do you think you could find out what's happened to Eefa before something really bad happens?"

"I'll find her!" beamed Luke, flinging open the door at the rear of the counter and racing up the stairs.

Resus and Cleo rolled their eyes, then followed.

"Thank you," said Luella, to no one in particular. She placed the remains of her spoon on the counter and blinked slowly. "I think I might go and have a lie-down."

Luke, Resus and Cleo crept along the dark corridor on the top floor of the emporium. The floorboards creaked beneath their feet.

"We need something to light the way," Luke whispered to Resus.

"Something light coming right up!" said the vampire, plunging his hand inside his magical cloak. He removed it clutching a feather.

"Well," he said, blushing, "it is *light*."

94

"Hurry up!" hissed Cleo.

Several useless objects later – a can of diet soda, a tub of make-up and a window pane – Resus finally produced a lit candle in a holder. The flame flickered orange, casting weird shadows along the walls.

"Come on," said Luke, taking the candle and leading the way.

They stopped at what they hoped was the door to Eefa's bedroom, and pushed it open with a *cccreeaakk!*

"Hello?" called Luke softly. "Eefa?"

The trio stepped into the darkened room. The windows had been blacked out with paint, and blankets were thrown over the mirrors.

"Looks just like my Auntie Olga's place," Resus pointed out.

"Eefa?" asked Cleo. "Are you here?"

A floorboard creaked, and the trio spun around to find the hideous hag from the attic portrait standing right behind them.

Resus squealed and jumped into Cleo's arms. "Aargh! Hideous portrait woman!"

The children backed up against the wall as the vision of ugliness advanced upon them.

 95

"Who are you?" demanded Luke, holding the candle out like a weapon in his trembling hand. "What have you done to Eefa?"

The vile vision opened her mouth, a long black tongue flicking over her few remaining teeth. "There's no need to be rude, Luke Watson," she said, in a very familiar voice.

"Eefa?" cried Luke and Cleo together.

Resus was still screaming.

"Oh, put a sock in it!" spat the witch.

Cleo dropped her friend to the ground.

"Aaaaaaarrrgghh!" Resus continued to cry out.

"Are you quite finished?" Luke asked.

"Hang on," replied Resus. "I'm nearly done... Aaaaaarrrgghh!" He paused to take a breath. "Right, finished," he said, climbing to his feet and brushing the dust from his trousers. "Now, Eefa, what in the name of Bram Stoker has happened to you?"

Chapter Four
THE DUMP

The ghastly face glared in anger. "*You* try to stay looking good for three hundred years without resorting to witchcraft," she grumbled.

Cleo slapped a bandaged palm to her head. "Let me guess. You kept an enchanted portrait of your true self in the attic, and that kept the physical you magically young."

"And then I threw the portrait out of the window!" added Luke.

"You did *what*?" screeched the bad-tempered

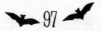

witch.

Luke paled. "Well, you see…"

"I told you *not* to touch anything on that side of the attic! Now, go and get it back before I turn you all into root vegetables!"

The trio turned and ran, the ugly Eefa hot on their tails. The cantankerous crone screeched to everyone in her way. "Out! Get out! The shop is closed!"

The emporium's customers took one look at the creature racing between the shelves and ran for their lives, screaming and crying.

Luke, Resus and Cleo grabbed Luella as they passed the counter and dragged her out into the street with them.

Eefa paused in the doorway and glanced up at the bat hanging above it. The animal gawped back, horrified.

"What are you staring at?" the witch shrieked, flinging the bat out into the open air.

Slam!

The door to Eefa's crashed closed.

The three friends found a nice quiet spot for the traumatised Luella, then raced around to the back of the emporium, where the bins were kept.

But the rubbish was gone.

"We're too late!" exclaimed Luke.

"What now?" demanded Resus.

"The town dump!" cried Cleo.

A long line of metal bins *clanked* and *banged* as they trundled along a conveyor belt. As the bins neared the end, a huge mechanical arm swooped down to pick them up and empty their contents into a vast smoking hole in the ground.

Luke, Resus and Cleo tottered along the conveyor belt, plunging their hands into the bins and rooting through their contents.

Cleo produced a foot. "Eww!"

"Bonus!" came a cry from a nearby mound of garbage. "You found it! Thanks, Cleo!"

The mummy tossed the foot down to its owner – Doug, the zombie.

Resus pulled an ear from the bin he was searching and did his best not to throw up. "I think this might be yours too, Doug," he said.

"You'll have to speak up, little vampire dude!" Doug yelled back. "I'm missing an ear!"

Resus tossed the ear to Doug and shuddered, wiping his hands on his cloak.

 99

"There!" cried Luke, pointing. "The painting!"

The others looked to see the painting of the old crone sticking out of a bin nearing the end of its journey. The mechanical arm was busy tipping the trash out of the receptacle right before it. If they didn't reach the bin very quickly...

Luke screwed his eyes closed and felt a familiar black sensation swoop through his body. He pushed the feeling down towards his feet. Soon the bones in his legs cracked and reformed as powerful muscles – and a thick coating of fur – rapidly grew.

Werewolf legs in place, he pounded along the conveyor belt, pushing bins out of the way as he ran. The arm dumped its current container and swung back towards the bin containing the portrait. Luke leapt for the painting and just managed to snatch it before the pincers of the mechanical arm clamped around his waist, and he was lifted into the air.

"Waaah!" he cried, as the machine swung him out over the burning pit.

Cleo pulled a length of bandage from her

waist, swung it around her head and tossed it towards Luke, just as the metal claw released its grasp and he plummeted down towards the deadly inferno below.

Luke stretched out an arm, and caught the bandage with his fingertips.

"Heave!" cried Cleo, and she and Resus hauled Luke to safety.

The trio slumped to the ground beside the fire pit, Luke's furry legs smouldering slightly. Doug lurched past on his reattached foot.

"Dudes!" he said, staring at the portrait. "No wonder you wanted to save it so bad; she's quite the looker!"

Luke glanced at the fiendish face then back to Doug, who leaned in and whispered: "I don't suppose you have her number, do you?"

Cleo brushed Luella's hair down to hide her missing eyebrows, while Luke and Resus hammered on the door to Eefa's.

"Come on, Eefa!" cried the vampire.

There was no reply.

Luke tried. "Eefa!" he called, sliding the canvas under the door. "We found your portrait!"

He smiled at a nervous Luella. "She'll be fine now, you'll see."

The door crashed open and Eefa glared out at them, still as revolting as ever.

Resus screamed again.

"You idiots!" spat the witch. "It's not the portrait that's magical. It's the frame! You have failed me!"

The door slammed shut again, and all the lights in the emporium went out.

"I need a hug!" wailed Luella.

Luke held his arms open.

"Not you," said the young witch, pushing past Luke to cuddle Resus. The vampire wrapped a reassuring arm around her. "We've got to find that frame," he said.

"Exactly," agreed Luke.

"But it could be absolutely anywhere," Cleo reminded them. "We can't just—"

"Keep up, Dixon!" bellowed a voice.

The four friends watched, open-mouthed, as Otto Sneer – or, rather, a new and improved version of Otto Sneer – jogged past. His glossy quiff waved in the air, revealing a young and handsome face beneath.

A few seconds later, Dixon staggered by, carrying a clutch of water bottles. He spotted the stunned expressions of his classmates and grinned. "Ever since Otto had that portrait done, he's a new man!"

Cleo reached out and grabbed Dixon's collar. "Wait a minute," she said. "You didn't help yourself to an old picture frame from the back of the shop earlier, did you?"

Otto stopped jogging and hid behind a tree to listen in.

"It's enchanted," said Luke. "And it belongs to Eefa."

Dixon opened his mouth to reply.

Quick as a flash, Otto streaked in and yanked Dixon from Cleo's grip. "Would love to stop and chat," he said, "but I've got a wash and blow-dry booked at five. Bye!"

The children could only watch as he dragged the exhausted shapeshifter away.

Back at Sneer Hall, Otto stood in the bathroom, holding his portrait. Taking a deep breath, he tore the picture from its frame. His full head of hair instantly disappeared.

"No!" he cried. "Come back, my beautiful bonce!"

He slipped the picture back into the frame and, *whoosh*, his good looks and hair were back in place.

Otto wrapped his arms around the portrait and cackled. "There's no way those kids are getting their grubby little hands on this!"

That night, Cleo spread a large papyrus scroll out on the grass beneath one of the windows of Sneer Hall. Luke pulled a torch from his pocket and clicked it on.

The plan on the scroll was written in hieroglyphics, and looked very, very complicated.

"Are we stealing a painting or overthrowing the entire Egyptian empire?" asked Resus.

Cleo ignored the comment. "OK, we enter through the roof, avoiding the security cameras, then we're in stealth-mode down the stairs and into the hall—"

"Or we could just go in that way," interrupted Luke, pointing to an open door.

Cleo glanced down at her complex plan of action.

"You can still forward-roll along the corridor, if you like," suggested Resus.

A few moments later, the trio crept across the vast room to where Otto's painting was hanging on the wall by a long piece of green string.

"That was easier than I expected," admitted Luke. But just as he reached out for the portrait, it shimmered and transformed into Dixon.

"Whoop-whoop-whoop!" Dixon yelled. "I'm an alarm now. Whoop-whoop!"

"You didn't think I'd let you steal my portrait that easily, did you?" snarled a voice. Otto Sneer emerged from a side door, accompanied by his huge, faceless henchman, NoName.

"You can keep your ugly portrait," snapped Cleo. "It's the frame we want."

"It belongs to Eefa," added Resus.

"She threw it away!" said Dixon, dropping down from where he'd been hanging on the wall. "Finders keepers!"

Luke stepped up to him and scowled. "We'll find it, wherever you've hidden it!"

Dixon scowled back. "Not if it's on the

105

Ghost Train headed to G.H.O.U.L. HQ in the normal world, you won't!"

"Dixon!" roared Otto.

"Oops!" exclaimed Dixon, clamping his hand over his mouth.

Luke turned to grin at Resus and Cleo. "Sorted."

Otto Sneer pushed past his assistant to stand nose-to-nose with Luke. "May I remind you, wolf boy, that the penalty for any Scream Street resident attempting to return to the normal world is ... banishment to the Underlands!"

The mayor turned to NoName. "Throw them out!"

Luke didn't blink. "You wouldn't dare!"

The trio landed in a pile on the grass outside.

"He dared," groaned Resus, untangling himself from his friends.

Back inside Sneer Hall, Otto removed the real painting and frame from his safe. "Get this to the Ghost Train," he ordered. "And double the security!"

"Right away, boss!" said Dixon, with a salute. Then his skin began to ripple as he shapeshifted into an identical copy of NoName.

Together, the two Movers marched away with the painting.

Chapter Five

THE GHOST TRAIN

Luke, Resus and Cleo hid in the bushes and watched as the two NoNames squeezed into one of the cars of the Ghost Train, along with the portrait of Otto Sneer and Eefa's magical frame. It clanked away into the dark tunnel that led to the normal world.

Bizarre, off-key circus music began to play.

"There it goes," said Resus.

Cleo sighed. "Poor Eefa."

"No," said Luke. "I'm not going to let this

happen." He closed his eyes tightly and began to wolf-up his legs again. "Eefa and I are the same; we've both got a side to us that we're ashamed of. Wish me luck!"

With that, he sprang out of the bushes, caught one of his long toe claws on a train rail and fell flat on his face.

"You might need to work on your heroic exits a bit," said Resus, helping him up.

"Please be careful," said Cleo. "You mustn't let them see you."

Luke winked at his friends, then raced into the tunnel at top speed.

Resus had an idea. "The invisibility sun-screen my mum bought!" he cried, pulling the bottle from his trouser pocket.

Cleo peered into the darkness of the Ghost Train tunnel. "Too late!"

"Not necessarily," said Resus, holding open one side of his cape. There, sleeping upside down, was Eefa's bat.

"Pssst! Wake up!" urged Resus. "Take this to Luke."

Blinking blearily, the bat took the bottle and flapped into the tunnel.

Luke's legs pumped hard as he raced along the tracks of the freaky fairground ride in the semi-darkness. Every now and then, a cardboard ghost or papier mâché spider leapt out at him, forcing him to duck or dodge to one side, the crazy music still blasting.

He spotted the last carriage of the Ghost Train up ahead, picked up speed to reach it, and leapt aboard. He landed with a *thump* on the floor of the carriage, and stayed hidden until he was certain that neither of the hulking henchmen were working their way back down the train to see what the noise was.

Cautiously, he peered over the front of the cart, grimacing as a fake spider's web brushed across his face. Up ahead, he could see the motionless Movers, with the magically framed picture nestled between them.

Slowly, he began to climb from carriage to carriage towards them.

Luke was just three carts behind when a plastic vampire dropped from the ceiling and made him jump. He caught his foot on the safety rail of the carriage with a *clang!* Instantly, Dixon and NoName spun around. Luke flattened himself against the seat, trying to control his breathing but ready to pounce if the need arose.

Peering through a gap in the wood, he watched NoName scan the rear of the train with whatever he used for eyes, then turn back and settle into his seat once more. Luke knew he would have to be more careful.

He stood, the stale air whipping across his face, and stepped carefully into the next carriage ahead. Now, he was just two carts behind the painting. He grabbed hold of the side rail to steady himself for his next move...

Clickety clack!

The Ghost Train rattled over the points that turned it from its current path and towards the exit into the real world. The whole train jerked violently to the left, sending Luke flying over the edge of the cart and heading for the tunnel wall.

Screwing his eyes shut, he transformed his left hand into that of his werewolf just in time, digging his long talons into the wooden panel of the carriage door and arresting his fall. Luke opened his mouth and screamed silently as he hung on for his life, body flapping in the breeze, the back of his head bumping against the rough tunnel wall.

After a moment, the tunnel arced right, and Luke was able to hook a foot over the side of the carriage. He dragged himself back inside the cart, where he sank to the floor, breathing hard. If he hadn't managed to transform his arm in time, he might have fallen directly beneath the wheels of the train.

Gritting his teeth, Luke stood again. He stepped into the next carriage, and then climbed into the cart directly behind Dixon and NoName.

The portrait was finally within his reach.

He stretched out a hand, fingers gripping the frame … and tugged gently.

But the picture was stuck fast between the two gargantuan goons. If he was going to pull it free, he would have to really go for it – without alerting its guards.

He reached out to make his snatch…

Flap! Flap! Flap!

Luke ducked, alerted by the new noise. Was it one of the Movers, clambering back to challenge him after witnessing his death-defying stunt? Or was this a new trick set up to scare passengers on the fairground ride?

He jumped as Eefa's bat landed softly on his shoulder and dropped the bottle of lotion into his lap.

"What's this?" he whispered to the bat. "I don't need protection from the sun in here, and Luella's mix doesn't work anyway. It makes you…" He grinned as the reason for the delivery fell into place.

Pulling out the cork with his teeth, he tipped a handful of gloop into his palm and began to rub it into his skin. "Tell Resus his idea is fantastic," he hissed, as the bat took to the air and flapped off into the shadows.

Dixon sat rigidly in his seat as the train rumbled forward. Then he spotted a small light glowing up ahead and smiled – it was the end of the line, and the exit into the normal world. Otto was going to be delighted that he had managed to complete a task without messing it up. In fact, as soon as they reached the approaching platform and the painting stopped hovering in the air, he would—

113

The painting was hovering in the air!

Dixon jumped to his feet and grabbed for it, making the cart sway and causing the real NoName's face to bump against the rough side of the tunnel. The henchman also jumped up and began to reach out for the floating frame.

Trying to stifle his laughter, the now-invisible Luke leapt back down the long line of carriages and dropped onto the track, still gripping Eefa's magical frame. He waved goodbye to Dixon and NoName, just as the anguished wails of the mayor's assistant blended in with the Ghost Train's whistle. The ride had arrived at its destination.

He cast one final glance at the circle of light that led back to his old life in the normal world, and set off running in the direction of Scream Street.

"There!" said Luke, as he tore Otto's portrait out of the magical frame and replaced it with the painting of the old crone. He stood his handiwork on the counter of the emporium and stepped back to study it.

114

The kids turned as they heard footsteps slowly heading down the stairs towards them.

"OMG! I can't, like, stand the tension!" cried Luella, disappearing into the stockroom.

Cleo crossed her bandaged fingers. "It will have worked, won't it?" she asked.

Resus shrugged. "If it hasn't, at least we won't have to deal with gooey old loved-up Luke any more."

Luke stuck out his tongue in his friend's direction, but didn't tear his eyes away from the staircase. It was a few moments before he realized that he was holding his breath.

"Ta-da!" said Eefa, emerging into the light. Her sleek blood-orange dress clung tightly to her figure, and her green eyes sparkled, setting off her alabaster skin and ruby lips. "I'm back – and about time, too!"

"What a relief!" blurted Luke. "I mean, not that I care… I would still like you no matter how you looked!"

Cleo was about to comment when the shop door crashed open, causing the bat hanging above it to shriek loudly. Otto Sneer raced in, followed closely by a very nervous Dixon.

"I knew you'd mess it up!" spat the mayor. "I just knew it!"

"But it wasn't my fault, boss!" Dixon whimpered. "I told you, the painting just floated away all by itself!"

Otto skidded to a halt in front of Eefa and looked her up and down. "Gah! If you look like that again, then I must..." He grabbed a silver tray from the counter and stared unhappily at his reflection. Everything was back to normal – the pockmarked complexion, the badly cared-for teeth and, worst of all, the thin, balding hair.

"Dixon!" he bellowed, dropping the tray.

"Yes, boss?"

"We must go to the beauty product aisle at once!"

As the mayor and his assistant made for the back of the shop, Eefa surveyed the mess left behind by Luella's attempts to mix potions for their customers.

"This place is a mess," she sighed. "I don't suppose anyone would like to help me tidy up a bit?"

Luke started to raise his arm, but Cleo grabbed it tightly, just as Resus grasped the other.

"Don't you dare," the mummy hissed in her friend's ear. Then she and Resus dragged Luke out of the shop.

The bat above the doorway shrieked happily.

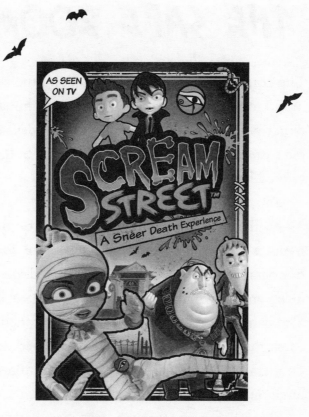

AN EXCERPT FROM THE NEW BOOK IN THE SERIES

Chapter One
THE SAFE ROOM

The zombie shuffled awkwardly along the street in the rain, one leg dragging behind as though it didn't want to go along with whatever depraved plan the undead creature had in mind. Still, the twisted limb kept pace.

Step, drag... Step, drag... Step, drag...

As the deluge of rain lashed down onto the monster's greasy, matted hair, an entire family of cockroaches washed free from the disgusting locks and down the zombie's pockmarked face. The beast stuck out its purple, bloated tongue to catch the unexpected treats, then crunched down on them, feeling them burst open. It continued to lurch onwards.

Striving to see through the torrential rain, the zombie's milky, leaking eyeballs eventually focused on a figure up ahead: a young boy, sitting innocently next to the open window of his living room, just three houses down. The creature twisted its mouth into what might have been a smile, then picked up speed.

The boy didn't see or hear the zombie as it limped closer. He was facing away from his stalker, lost in the antics of a popular presenter on the screen in front of him. The monster reached out and grabbed his shoulder with long-nailed fingers, pus oozing freely from the open sores that covered the gripping hand.

"Doug!" cried Luke Watson, spinning round to face his zombie friend. "How's it going?"

"Totally righteous, little dude!" beamed the creature, flicking his limp, wet hair away from his eyes. "I'm just out for my morning constitutional."

Luke's eyes flicked up to the churning grey clouds that filled the sky. "Not ideal weather for it," he said. "Do you want to come in, out of the rain?"

"Thanks, but no thanks, old pal," Doug replied. "Can't beat a good downpour to wash the bed bugs out of your brain. I hope it lasts."

"Let's find out," said Luke, snatching up a wand and flicking it in front of the magic mirror on the wall. The game show he had been watching — called *The Price is Fright* — disappeared, and a zombie weather reporter appeared in its place.

"Hey, that's Mitch Flesh!" cried Doug. "My favourite!"

The pair watched as the weatherman finished his report: "... the stormy conditions are set to continue, with intermittent hail, thunder and lightning. In summary, it's another beautiful day in Scream Street!"

"Hail?" mused Doug, peering upwards. "I haven't noticed any—"

Before the zombie could finish his sentence, huge hailstones the size of potatoes began to clatter down from the sky. Doug yelped as the massive balls of ice pummelled him to the ground.

"Are you OK?" asked Luke, once the shower had subsided and it was safe to stick his head out of the window again.

"Never better, dude," groaned the zombie, struggling to lift his battered body out of the mud. "At least it wasn't the—"

Crrrraaassshhh!

An electric blue bolt of lightning rocketed from the churning clouds and smashed straight into Doug's chest. Luke fell back off the sofa, his vision burning from the flash of light. He scrambled back up, rubbing his eyes, and was amazed to find

 122

Doug not only upright, but also dancing in the rainstorm.

"Wahey!" cackled the cavorting corpse. "Now *that's* got the old engine running!" The zombie paused to lick his lips. "I think I might go find a party that's in need of some Doug."

Luke shook his head as Doug leapt over the garden fence and hurried away. Then he turned his attention back to the magic mirror, just as the weather zombie grabbed a handful of his own hair and ripped off his head. Tossing the bonce aside, the body reached beneath the newsdesk for a replacement – this one female – and stuck it onto the exposed piece of spine jutting out between its shoulders.

"Thanks, Mitch," said the newly nogginned newscaster. "Coming up: Crazed resident banished to the Underlands."

Luke leaned towards the screen as the image changed to footage of yet another zombie, this one being dragged towards a fiery portal by NoName, the mayor of Scream Street's huge hired henchman.

"No!" the crazed creature yelled. "I'll be good! I promise!"

NoName hesitated at the edge of the portal. The monstrous minder didn't have a face, just an expanse of smooth skin, so it was impossible to tell quite what he was thinking. Luke imagined he was considering giving the convicted criminal a second chance. The Underlands were the dreaded land beneath Scream Street, where monsters were sent when they turned on their neighbours.

Suddenly, the zombie lunged for NoName's leg, teeth bared. But the bulging bodyguard was too quick. Shoving two massive fingers up the zombie's nostrils, he flicked the miscreant, still screaming for mercy, through the portal of fire and down into the terrifying world below.

Luke shuddered as the picture switched back to Anna Gored, the newsreader.

"Lastly," she said with a twisted smile, "a reminder for all residents that there will be a special announcement at today's town meeting. Attendance at the meeting is, as ever, compulsory. Absentees will be strung up in the town square by their—"

"Luke!" cried a voice from upstairs.

Luke grabbed the wand and turned off the magic mirror. "Yes, Mum?"

"Time for the safe-room drill!"

"Oh, no," said Luke to himself as he headed for the stairs. "Not this again."

Ever since moving to Scream Street, Luke's parents had been searching for a way to keep themselves safe whenever their son transformed into his werewolf. They'd tried locking him inside a cage once, but quickly discovered that the wolf was strong enough to bend the bars.

They'd also tried chains, only to find that the lengths of metal gave Luke's werewolf a handy weapon to wield in addition to its teeth and claws.

So, Mike Watson had set about building a safe room – a sealed vault that he and his wife, Sue, could lock themselves into whenever Luke "went a bit wolfy". There had, however, been teething problems, and Mike and Sue had decided to initiate a series of tests whenever the safe room was upgraded.

Luke found his dad at the top of the stairs, tongue sticking out of his mouth as he concentrated on fitting an elaborate new lock to the inside of the safe-room door.

"Ready, dear?" asked Sue, as Luke reached the landing.

"Ready as I'll ever be!" Luke said, forcing a smile.

"Right!" said Mike, tucking the screwdriver into his pocket. "Let's see how long it takes your mother and me to lock ourselves inside my new and improved safe room."

Nobody moved.

"What are you waiting for?" Luke asked.

"Motivation!" cried Mike. "The room might be ready to keep us safe from your wolf's pointy bits – but I'm not really feeling the fear, if you get my meaning."

Luke rolled his eyes. In their old life, Mike had been a long-standing member of the local amateur dramatic society, a passion he'd not yet found an outlet for in Scream Street.

"OK," Luke sighed. He held up his hands to look like paws. "Roar."

"No, no, no!" exclaimed Mike. "Where's the terror? Where's the anger? Where's the wolf?"

"What, you actually want me to transform?" Luke asked.

"Oh good gracious no!" said his father quickly. "I just want you to give your performance a little more ... bite, shall we say.

Now, once more, with feeling."

This time, Luke closed his eyes and dug down, deep inside himself. He pictured the first time he had ever transformed in public, when he had been trying to protect an innocent classmate from a beating by a school bully. He remembered how it had felt when the bully turned on him instead. How each blow had pushed him closer and closer to setting the werewolf free...

"Rrroooaaaarrrrrr!"

Mike squealed in terror as Luke raced towards him. He grabbed his wife's hand, pulled her inside the safe room, and slammed the door. Instantly, the new lock activated, metal scraping against metal as the heavy bolts locked into place.

Bang! Clunk! Thump!

"There!" said Mike, when he could catch his breath. "Perfect!"

"Ahem."

Mike shrieked and jumped into his wife's arms. Luke was standing inside the safe room with them. "I'm pretty sure you're not supposed to let the werewolf in here with you," he said with a grin.

Sue gently lowered her husband to the ground.

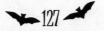

"I guess we need to be a little quicker," she said, checking her watch. "But there's no time for a rerun now. We don't want to be late for the town meeting."

Retracting the bolts, she flung the door open and led her still-trembling husband down the stairs. Luke made to follow, until his foot clanked against something on the ground. The new handle had fallen off the back of the door.

"Hey, Dad!" he called, bending to pick it up. "You didn't screw this in prop—"

Click!

The reinforced door to the safe room swung shut. Luke gave it a push. It was locked tight.

"Seriously?" he groaned.